GO WITH
THE MOON

GO WITH THE MOON

WRITTEN AND ILLUSTRATED BY
JONNA DOREEN MAGNUSSEN

Library of Congress Control Number: 2021914238
ISBN: 978-17375719-0-2

Edited by Amy Perez
Illustrations painted in acrylics
All animals named by Miss Eva Doreen

This is my little brother.

He's a bit afraid of the dark.

But don't worry.

I am not scared.

I just go with the moon.

Take my hand.

We'll be there soon.

What's that?

What's that sound?

Oh, my goodness!

Who's coming around?

Don't worry little brother.
That's just my friend,
Lovey the Fox.
Lovey, come closer.
Meet my little brother.

WOAH,

NOT THAT CLOSE!

Back it up,

little buddy.

There you go sweet boy!
Much Better.

Come on little brother.
Just go with the moon.
Take my hand,
we'll be there soon.

What's that?
What's that sound?
What's that light?
Who's coming around?

Don't worry little brother.
That's just our friend,
Glowy the Glow Worm.
Sorry Little Lady,
so sorry to disturb you.

Come on little brother,
just go with the moon.
Take my hand,
we'll be there soon.

Who's that?
What's that sound?
Hooooooooo Hooooooooo,
who's coming around?

Don't worry little brother.
Those hoooooooos
are coming from
Owly and Prowly,
the owl sisters.

Good night my owl friends.

Come on little brother,
just go with the moon.
Take my hand,
we'll be there soon.

What's that in the bushes?
What's that sound?
Rustling and Crackling.
Who's coming around?

Don't worry little brother.
Beardy the Great and Wise
resides here.
He watches over the hills and
keeps out the crawlies.
Sweet escapades my wily friend.

Come on little brother.
Just go with the moon.
Take my hand,
we'll be there soon.

Oh my, what's that?
What's that sound?
Crashing and Dashing,
who's coming around?

Don't worry little brother.
It's just Catchy the Cat
trying to catch
Cheesy the Mouse
as a late-night snack.

He's a bit too fat
and she's a bit too fast
and so it goes around and around,
she'll be safe at last.

Come on little brother,
just go with the moon.
Take my hand,
we'll be there soon.

Ahhhhh, above us!
What's that sound?
Flapping and Screeching,
who's flying around?

Don't worry little brother,
this is Batty the Bat.
She won't eat us.
She just wants slugs
and jugs of beetle bugs.

Come on little brother,
just go with the moon.
Take my hand,
we'll be there soon.

Are we almost there?
What's that?
What's that sound?
Look at those prints,
who's going around?

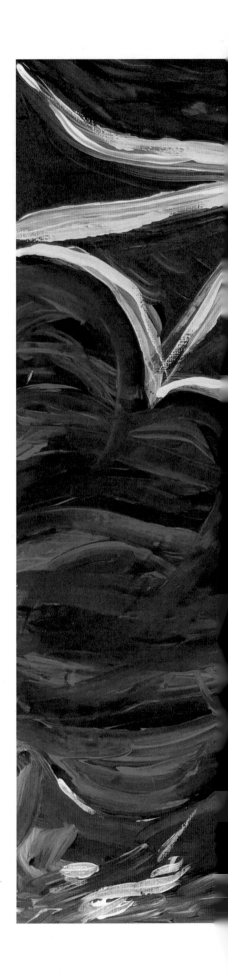

Quick follow those prints!
Looks like
Goaty the Goat
and Swingy the Monkey
got into the
ginseng peppermint.

Up all night,
jumping and swinging,
they can follow us too,
and go with the moon.

Come on little brother,
just go with the moon.
Take my hand,
we'll be there soon.

What's that?
What's that sound?
Oh, my goodness!
Who's coming around?

Don't worry little brother.
Howdy!
This is Trashy the Raccoon.
Lead the way,
Little Lady.
Up this Way!

Come on little brother.
Just go with the moon.
Take my hand.
We'll be there soon.

Under the cottonwood.

Under the moon.

No need to be afraid.

Just go with the moon.

Jonna Doreen lives in the Flint Hills of North East Kansas with her husband and three children. Born and raised in El Paso, Texas, she moved to Kansas to raise her family. She gardens, paints, and explores the wilderness of Beautiful Kansas.

Made in the USA
Monee, IL
10 April 2023

31390173R00024